MIDDLE SISTER

Also by Eric Williford

The Dead Ate Cheese
The Big Decay
Rich People $hit

CONTENTS

ONE

"The fucker's hiding in plain sight—he's practically begging for it." Val scoffed and bit a chunk out of the Snickers bar. She leaned against the black van as her teeth mashed the nougat, caramel, peanuts, and chocolate. For as long as Tessa could remember, Val had carried her weight like it was everyone else's burden.

The convenience store was so close to the highway it forced the sisters to raise their voices whenever a truck whizzed by. One of the streetlights flickered—a subtle warning not to proceed with this plan.

Tessa took a swig of her blue Gatorade—the sugar-free one. She had acquired the taste while running track at Temple. Her high school coach had urged her to try the middle distances. Her slim frame and speed were more suited for the 800. His words, not hers. She wasn't fast in the gifted way. She wasn't blessed with God-given speed to compete in the 100 or 200. But the eight hundred was as much about will power as it was about speed.

A year after graduating with a communications degree, she was standing in this convenience store parking lot with her two sisters, trying to muster the courage to close out the last leg of this trek and do the business they came to do.

The liquor store was only an hour away.

They had already been on the road for three hours.

"It's not too late for us to turn around. Forget all this," Esme said, her eyes fixed on the open bag of salt and vinegar potato chips resting in her hand. Of the three sisters, Esme's skin tone was the closest to their mother's—dark brown and flawless, accompanied by sad, brown eyes. Esme had always been bookish, often preferring solitude over the random adventures her older sisters had always dragged her into.

"There's no turning back now. This is what Mother wanted, so this is what we're doing." Val crammed the rest of the candy bar into her mouth and let the wrapper drift to the ground.

"You're not gonna litter, are you?" Tessa's tone was stern. Being the middle sister had taught her that when dealing with her older sister, showing strength was a must.

After a brief eye roll, Val stooped and took hold of the wrapper. "Happy?"

Tessa made her way to the van. "We need to get there before closing time."

Since she was little, Tessa had loved road trips. The open road and the sense of adventure made her blood rush. When her parents told her she could go to college anywhere within a six-hour drive, she picked Temple. It was the furthest school within the six-hour range. They also offered her a partial track scholarship.

The van was a rental—a black cargo van made for shady operations. Val drove and Tessa sat beside her.

In the back seat, Esme stared out the window.

"When we get there," Val said, "we should go in, do a little recon."

Tessa glared at her sister. "Recon?"

"You know. To make sure it's him."

Esme leaned forward and whispered, "Without the masks?"

Val stole a quick glance at Esme. "We'll go in like regular customers. Just some girls wanting to buy vodka or whatever."

Tessa sighed. "If we go in, we'll be on camera without our masks."

"I don't like this," Esme said. "The whole point of the mask is to hide our faces."

"Jesus." Val tightened her grip on the steering wheel. "I'm only suggesting this to put you at ease. You're the one worried about us grabbing the wrong guy."

Tessa pulled out a faded picture from the late 1990's. It was one of those photographs from a disposable camera with the loud turning mechanism you rotated in order to roll the film. It was of a smiling clean-shaven man staring straight at the camera. His smile was wide and unnerving. Even in the faded picture, his perfectly tanned skin seemed to glow. The paintings on the wall behind him were cheap drip-paint abstracts, created by a poor man's Jackson Pollock. The guy's eyes made Tessa uneasy. Maybe it was the knowledge of what he did.

Or maybe it was knowing what she and her sisters were about to do.

"What's your verdict?" Val took her eyes off the road long enough to silently let Tessa know how she expected her to answer.

"As long as we don't do anything crazy without our masks, we should be fine." Tessa passed the picture back to Esme.

Esme studied the man in the photograph. "Hard to believe this guy is capable of all those things."

Val's voice was laced with a barely contained rage. "He is, and he's gonna pay."

Ever since her breakup, Val had been a volcano looking for any excuse to erupt and burn anyone in her path. For the most part, Tessa did her best to avoid her, but in the last couple of months, it'd been even harder to keep her distance. Esme, who still lived in the house, received the brunt of it.

"You know this guy is gonna be like fifty or sixty now." Esme passed the picture back to Tessa. "Are we gonna know it's him?"

"We'll know it's him." Tessa's voice was comforting, even though her heart sank as the van passed the sign reading *Welcome to Allentown*. The sign was like a doomsday warning. Nothing would ever be the same from here on out.

Talking about it was one thing, but were they ready for this? It was all too real.

Allentown was located on the Lehigh River. Tessa had only driven through the miniature city on her way to track meets. She never gave it much thought. Even now it was nothing more than a random place they should be in and out of in less than two hours.

The liquor store was situated in the middle of a strip mall, wedged between a dry cleaners and a sandwich shop. Half of the remaining stores were boarded shut, begging for a new investor, or a mercy demolition.

Val maneuvered the van to the back corner of the parking lot, as far away from the liquor store as possible.

Tessa checked her watch. "He should be closing in twenty minutes."

Esme whispered, "Looks like the other stores have already closed for the night."

In an instant, Val unbuckled her seatbelt and opened the van door. "Time for some recon." She didn't wait for a response, and slammed the door shut behind her.

Tessa and Esme followed her out. The wind came in off the Lehigh

River and added to the wind chill factor. Tessa kept her head lowered so she didn't have to face the breeze head on.

Val was the first to enter the liquor store. Tessa swallowed as she crossed the threshold. The neon beer and liquor signage casting the store in a haze of artificial blues and reds. Her throat was dry, like she was on the verge of a sore throat, but she knew it was nerves. The bearded guy behind the register hardly acknowledged them.

Esme's nervous energy slammed against Tessa's back. Val settled in by the bottles of vodka, making a show of holding one in a not-so-subtle attempt to stare at the guy behind the register. When the other two sisters arrived, Val whispered, "That's him. One hundred percent."

Tessa's eyes met his. He was the right age. The facial hair made it tough to gauge his features. They stared at each other for an eternity, until he said, "I'm closing in ten. If you got questions, let me know."

Val said, "Is this all the vodka?"

"Yep." He turned his attention back to his crossword puzzle.

Val turned her back to the man and faced her sisters. With her big brown eyes as wide as saucers, she mouthed the words, *That's him.*

When Val was this certain about an idea, there was no convincing her otherwise. She had always been the most stubborn of the sisters. It didn't matter what Tessa said, or how much Esme protested. They were going through with the plan, and this was their guy.

Even if he wasn't their guy.

Tessa brushed past her older sister and headed straight for the door. "You don't have what we're looking for. Thanks, though." His low-cut beard was grey and his eyes were tired. Not from a late night at work. These eyes belonged to a man who was tired of life. Exhausted from decades of making the wrong choices at every turn. Tessa barged out the door.

It was him. It had to be.

Halfway to the van, Val nearly caught her sister. "It was him, wasn't it?"

"I believe so."

At the van, Esme arrived behind them.

Val grinned. "Great. Let's get changed." She opened the back door and they climbed in.

As the van door slammed shut, Tessa opened the duffel bag, pulled out a white coverall, and tossed it to Esme. Val was already undressed, in nothing but her bra and underwear by the time Tessa handed her the second white coverall.

Esme stared at the white coverall in her hand.

Tessa shimmied out of her jeans and pulled her t-shirt over her head. "Clothes in the bag." Val crammed her clothes into the duffel bag as Tessa stepped into the coveralls.

Esme stepped out of her jeans. She moved with half the urgency of her sisters.

"Get the masks." Tessa zipped herself into the coveralls as Val pulled out three masks.

Val noticed Esme's reluctance; her voice was more exhausted than angry. "What's the holdup, girl?"

Esme slipped one leg into the coveralls, followed by the other. She stood and slowly zipped the coveralls. The moment she finished, Val shoved the pig mask into her hand. Esme studied it. "Why do I have to be the pig?"

Tessa could see that Val was ready to blow a gaskct. "It doesn't matter. I'll be the pig." She took two steps towards Esme, but stopped when Val snatched the pig mask from her.

"I'll be the damn pig. You be the bunny." Val handed Esme the bunny mask and tossed the fox mask to Tessa. "We happy?"

"No names from here on out." Tessa pointed to Esme. "You're Bunny." Then she pointed at Val. "You're Piggy. And I'm Foxy."

Val slipped the piggy mask over her face and made her way to the front of the van for a better view of the store front.

Tessa slid the mask over her face and turned to Esme. "It's a good plan. We'll be fine as long as we stick together."

Esme slid the mask over her face.

And the sisters waited. Tessa worked retail back in high school. She had already briefed her sisters on what he'd have to do before leaving. Count out the register. Sweep the floor. Check the shelves to make sure the bottles are straight. The last part of his checklist would be to take out the trash and lock up. If he was good, he would be out in under an hour. If he was in a rush, it may only take him twenty minutes.

Thirty minutes later, Val turned back to her sisters. "He's out. It's go time."

Tessa pulled a tascr out of the backpack.

Val opened the back door and the sisters burst out. They raced across the parking lot, with Val in front. When the cashier noticed them, it was too late. Val greeted him with a left hook to his chin. The shock of the blow staggered him long enough for Tessa to tase him. Electricity surged through him. His body seized for a moment before going limp.

Esme grabbed the man's legs, while Val scooped him under the shoulders. Tessa sprinted back to the van and opened the back door as her sisters carried the limp body, tossing him in. He was barely under six feet tall, so his feet dangled out the back of the van. Val jumped out the back door, made her way to the front, and jumped in behind the wheel. Esme pushed the man's legs inside the van, climbed in, and shut the door.

Tessa already had the zip ties out and used them to bind the man's hands and feet.

Esme tore a strip of duct tape off the roll and used it to cover his mouth, then draped a burlap sack over his head.

Val yelled, "We good?"

Tessa took a moment to admire her and Esme's work. "Yeah." She opened the back door and let Esme out before stepping out herself. The two made their way to the front of the van. Tessa slumped into the passenger seat and Esme got in behind her sisters.

The engine sputtered to life, and Val peeled out of the parking lot.

Two

Streetlights on the sides of the highway blurred as the van sped into the darkness. Tessa glanced at the speedometer, confident they were going a hundred miles an hour. "Watch your speed, Val."

"I've been thinking," Val said, ignoring Tessa. "We should get a confession out of him first."

Vintage Val—all fire and brimstone at first, but after some time alone with her thoughts, she always surrendered to the more rational way of doing things. But of course, she would never apologize. She did what she always did: frame her apology in a way that made it seem like it was her idea—a profound revelation only she could have had.

Val continued, "He needs to confess to what he did all those years ago. Admit who he is, and confess what he did so we know we did the right thing."

Tessa's eyes stayed glued to the darkness in front of them. "Can you slow the hell down? The last thing we need right now is to get pulled over."

"Should we be talking about this now?" Esme's voice quivered. "He's literally right behind us."

Val chuckled. "Tessa filled him full of electricity. He won't be awake for hours."

Through gritted teeth, Tessa said, "Slow down, Val. Christ!"

"Okay. Sorry. Jesus." Val eased her foot off the accelerator and the van dropped about ten miles per hour. "But seriously. How about it?"

Tessa paused. "I'm not interested in killing a random guy."

"Are we admitting..." Esme let her breath catch in her throat, "that we may have the wrong guy?"

"I swear, you take everything to defcon three." Val tightened her grip as if it would help her quell the urge to rip her sister's throat out.

Tessa turned to her sister with a forced smile for reassurance. "All we're trying to do is make sure we're doing the right thing before we cross the point of no return."

"So we're clear," Esme said. "We're not a hundred percent sure this is the guy."

"He's the right guy." Tessa turned to Val. "Right?"

Val kept her eyes on the road, unaware Tessa was speaking to her. When the silence got obvious, she blurted out, "Yeah. He's the guy. But still. We should get a confession."

"Jesus." Esme flopped back into her seat with an overdramatic sigh.

"We'll get the confession," Tessa said.

"You know, Esme," Val said. "If you want out, we can pull over and you can get the fuck out."

Tessa turned to gaze outside the window. "Val—"

"I'm just saying."

"If I wanted to get out, you'd pull over and let me out." Esme let loose a mocking laugh doubling as a challenge.

Before Val could reply, the man groaned.

The sisters fall silent.

He groaned a second time.

Esme leaned forward and whispered, "You said he'd be out for hours."

"It's fine." Val, cool as can be, continued, "All we have to do is fill him with some more voltage. Foxy, you wanna do the honors?"

"I saw a sign for a rest stop. Pull in and I'll take care of it." Tessa straightened her back and readied herself.

Val pulled into the first rest stop they came across and eased the van into a parking space. It was scarcely populated with vans and trucks. A remnant from a bygone era, the only building was a restroom with a few vending machines lining the outer wall. Before Tessa could open the door, Val whispered, "Hold on a sec."

Tessa's body tensed. She glanced out Val's window as two patrol cars entered the rest area. One of them parked beside the van, while the other took a spot on the opposite side.

Panic rose in Esme's voice. "Are they here for us?"

Val shushed her between gritted teeth.

An officer stepped out of each patrol car. Without as much as a glance at the van, they leaned against their cars and chatted.

"What in the actual fuck?" Val closed her eyes and counted to three.

Panic rose in Esme's voice. "I say we back out and hit the road?"

"They're on break or whatever. They had to have seen us pull in. If we leave without using the facilities, they'll get suspicious." Tessa mulled it over for a moment and added, "I'll go pee."

"No. Esme will go. You stay here. If the cops leave, you stick the guy with the taser."

"Why do I have to go?" Esme protested.

"Does it need to be a debate?" Val's counting exercise had failed her. Her infamous temper was bubbling to the surface."

"Fine. I'll go." Esme let herself out of the van and stomped across the parking lot. The officers allowed themselves a moment to watch her.

Tessa raised her eyebrows. "Are they checking out her ass or wondering why the hell she's wearing a white jumpsuit?"

Val snorted. "Probably both."

Esme vanished into the ladies' room and the officers resumed their discussion on whatever it is they were talking about.

The man groaned again.

Val immediately turned to see if the officers heard him.

They didn't.

Using her eyes, Tessa motioned for Val to turn the radio up. The decimals rose and Leon Bridges filled the van.

The cops glanced at the van. Val responded with a forced smile and a half-hearted wave. The officers rolled their eyes and resumed their discussion.

"Here she comes." Tessa watched through the mirror as Esme hustled across the parking lot. "What now?"

"We leave the moment she gets in."

"What about the guy?" Tessa asked.

Val drummed her fingers on the steering wheel. "We'll pull over once we get on the highway."

Esme got into the van, and Val threw it in reverse. Without looking, Tessa knew the cops were watching them as they pulled onto the freeway ramp.

Two miles away from the rest stop, Val pulled the van onto the shoulder of the highway. The man's groans had become more frequent. More urgent. Tessa put her mask back on and got out. There wasn't a car in sight as she opened the back door and got in.

The man fought against his binds and pushed himself against the side of the van. Tessa pulled the taser out of the duffel bag.

He tried to speak, but the duct tape muffled his speech.

Tessa turned on the taser and stuck it into his rib cage. She held it against him as his body shook and contorted. After nearly ten seconds, she removed the taser. The man's body slumped. After a moment, the smell hit her and she gagged. Her forearm covered her nostrils as her eyes watered. The smell meant one thing.

The taser stayed in her hand as she exited the van and got back in her seat. "Let's go."

Val used her thumb and pointer finger to pinch her nose shut. "He shit himself, didn't he?"

"Yeah," Tessa said as she rolled her window down.

"We can't keep doing this to him. It's torture," Esme said.

Val pulled the van back onto the highway. "He deserves what he gets."

If this thing went south, it'd be because Val and Esme couldn't keep from tearing each other apart. Through the years, Tessa had seen Val and Esme turn family holidays into ash just to prove one was right and the other was wrong. The two had come to blows on numerous occasions. Most of the time, Tessa had been the one to settle it. But once she left for college, things between Esme and Val had gotten exponentially worse. Without the voice of reason, the two of them found new and innovative ways to rip each other apart.

Mother only exasperated things. Until the diagnosis.

Once they got the news about their mother, the sisters rallied to her side. Tessa came home, and an unspoken peace treaty was found. But this revenge plot seemed to be putting a strain on their newfound camaraderie.

Coming home wasn't all about caring for their mother. The post-graduation job market had been brutal. Tessa had gone on numerous interviews. So many she lost count. But no real offers had come through, at least nothing to be considered as the foundation of a career. Instead, she bounced around. Bartended at a few places. Made lattes at a few others. A week after getting fired from a hole-in-the-wall coffee shop that featured a rotation of guest DJ's, Tessa heard the news about their mother. Her liver was failing and she didn't have much time left.

Tessa was home two days later and slept in the same room she grew up in. Even the stuffies were right where she left them. Being back in the house with her sisters was comforting. But it didn't quell the constant poke of failure.

Always there.

Always chiding her.

The funeral had helped take her mind off her failures. As always, Valerie took the lead moments after their mother had passed on. They were hardly out of the hospital before Val was assigning duties to her younger sisters. Tessa didn't mind. She had grown accustomed to Val's commands and barked orders. It was easier to go with it. *Play your part and let Val act like the leader.*

It was Esme who fought Val whenever possible.

Val said closed casket.

Esme wanted it open.

Val wanted a small ceremony, with only a few of their mother's closest friends and family.

Esme wanted to invite everyone who had ever spoken to her.

Tessa negotiated a compromise. More people than Val said they could afford. Less people than what Esme thought their mother deserved.

At times, it was easier to leave them both disappointed.

It was at the funeral they met their mother's friends. The two women who their mom kept secret from her daughters. The two women who would set them on their current path.

Three

Built by former slaves who had migrated north after the Civil War, the farmhouse was a relic of a bygone era. Passed from generation to generation, it stood as a symbol of perseverance. Even now, with its patchwork roof, mismatched shutters, and overgrown acreage, the sisters were proud to call this place home.

Arguments about what to do with the farmhouse had begun hours after the wake. Their mother had willed the property to the sisters, same as it had been passed to her by their grandfather. Esme, always looking for an escape, had wanted to sell the property and split the money three ways.

Val wasn't having any of it. Tessa stood by, cleaning the food off the table as her sisters tore into each other. When the insults got personal, Tessa changed the subject. She decided to ask them about the two women who came to pay their respects—the women kept hidden from them.

One could argue this entire fiasco was Tessa's fault.

Val parked the van behind the house, close to the shed. The farmhouse was secluded and shrouded in darkness. Moonlight drew attention to the overgrown grass and brush. Crickets chirped and a cool breeze whipped across the property. They stepped out of the van and closed the doors behind them, their masks already on. Esme the bunny, Val the pig, and Tessa the fox. They met at the back of the van and Val threw the doors open. In the darkness, Tessa could hardly make out the figure of the man on the floor. Her eyes watered from the stench of hour old feces she assumed had begun to harden in the man's underwear. Tessa slid the duffel bag towards Esme.

Their captive remained passed out. Val handed the keys to Esme and motioned for her to open the shed.

Tessa looped her arms around the man's shoulders and hoisted his upper body. Val grabbed his legs, and together, the two women carried him towards the end of the van. Tessa had to stoop and slide her butt along the floor and lowered herself out without dropping him.

Once they were out, they shuffled across the ankle high grass towards the shed, where Esme had the door open and waiting. Tessa struggled with the man's weight and the awkwardness of carrying him by the shoulders with his head against her chest. His height was above average, and his weight had to be around two twenty. Val, with her arms holding his legs on either side of her waist, backed into the dark shed. Once Tessa crossed the threshold, Esme closed the door behind them and rushed over to pull the string to turn on the single bulb hanging from the ceiling.

Val grumbled at her younger sister as the bulb awakened with three blinks before it illuminated the single chair in the middle of the shed.

Muscle fatigue streaked through Tessa's shoulders as she carried the man around to the back of the chair and hoisted him into a sitting position, resulting in an audible squish as his ass settled into his excrement filled pants.

Tessa turned her head and fought back the vomit erupting in her throat. When she turned back around, Val had already cut the zip ties, freeing his hands. Esme handed her replacement ties and they used them to fasten his arms to the chair.

Val kneeled and freed the man's legs, using new zip ties around his ankles to bind him to the legs of the chair.

Rusted garden tools crowded the walls and the work bench in the back of the shed. There was barely enough room for the four of them.

Tessa's Gatorade flavored breath added a humidity to the inside of her plastic fox mask, thickening the stench from the man's soiled underwear. Between the closed door and the lack of windows, the aroma of warm feces permeated the thick, sweaty air.

Esme motioned to the door. "I need some air."

"Don't." Val's tone was sharp and authoritative.

Esme froze in her tracks. "He's still passed out. What are we going to do?"

Without a word, Val calmly strutted over to the man, leaned over, and ripped off the duct tape covering his mouth. After nearly four hours, the glue from the tape had adhered to the man's face, causing some of his stubble to come off. His skin was left so raw, the only thing remaining was a red outline in the shape of the tape.

The man's eyes opened in a panic. For the first time since the initial kidnapping, the sisters got a chance to see the terror they caused as he pleaded. "What… what is this?"

Val rose to her feet, casting an intimidating shadow over the helpless man. "What's your name?"

Words sputtered out of his mouth like a clogged faucet. "Why… why do you want to know?"

"Answer her." Tessa's voice, distorted from the mask, rang out from behind him.

"You kidnap me..." The man struggled to keep his composure. "And you don't even know my name."

"We want to hear you say it." In a theatrical display worthy of a SAG award, Val turned her back to the man and studied the nail gun hanging on the wall.

Tessa lowered her hands onto his shoulders and gave them a squeeze. "It's okay. Go ahead and tell us."

"You electrocuted me." His voice downshifted to a whisper. "You made me shit my pants."

Val spoke without turning from the nail gun. "We'll do much worse if you're not honest with us."

Sweat mixed with the smell of shit added a layer of sweetness to the foul aroma. The only sound was the man's heavy breathing.

"We're gonna get the truth out of you, one way or another." Val turned to face him, the single light source carving her pig mask out of the darkness.

"Gregory."

Tessa squeezed his shoulders again. "Have you ever gone by another name, Gregory?"

"What do you mean, another name?"

Tessa released her grip and made her way around to face him. "Maybe a long time ago. Did people call you by another name?"

"Greg. People sometimes call me Greg." His attention turned from Tessa to the woman in the pig mask taking the nail gun from the wall.

Under the mask, Tessa pinched her lips together. "You know what name we're talking about."

"I have no idea what you're talking about. Or why I'm here. I work in a damn liquor store. I'm a nobody."

Val tested the weight of the nail gun in her hand. "Everyone is someone to somebody."

"You're someone to us, and we need you to admit it," Tessa added, sweat from her forehead making its way into her left eye. She blinked to try and ease the sting.

His eyes darted from one tool to another. Stains formed in the pits of his shirt. "I'm not the guy you're looking for. I swear it."

"If you tell us who you were many years ago," Tessa let the pause hang in the air before continuing, "it'll make all of this quicker for us, and less painful for you."

"Who I was years ago? What the hell are you talking about?"

Val pointed the nail gun at his head. "You know exactly what we're talking about."

The man's eyes locked in on the nail gun. Snot poured from his nose and his upper lip quivered. "Take all my money. I don't have much, but it's yours. Please. Take it and let me go."

Val pressed the nail gun against his forehead. "Does this feel like a robbery to you?"

"I don't… I don't know."

Tessa leaned into his face and whispered, "Brother John." She studied his vacant eyes full of confusion. "Ring a bell?"

The man kept his eyes on the barrel of the yellow and black nail gun. "No."

Val tilted her head to the side. "Yeah, you do."

"No, I don't." The man struggled to contain his whimpers. "Are you… saying I'm a guy named Brother John?"

Val's words were calm and calculating. "You may not be him now, but you were him at one point in time."

"You've got the wrong guy. I swear it."

Tessa made her way to Val. "Well, Piggy, he needs to be taught the punishment for lying."

Val pulled the nail gun away from the man's head and aimed it at his left hand perched on the wooden arm of the chair. "When you lie to us, you force us to hurt you." The air crackled with a hiss as a nail discharged from the gun into the man's hand, through the wood, and out the bottom. The top of the nail was barely visible in his hand. Blood gushed out and splattered against the floor.

The man wailed in agony.

The door to the shed slammed shut. Esme was gone.

Four

Val snarled at Tessa. "What the hell is she doing?" The nail gun shook in her hand as her focus began to waver.

"I'll get her." Tessa was halfway to the door when the final word left her lips.

"I'm going with you." Val turned to the man in the chair. "Don't go anywhere."

By the time Tessa stepped out of the shed, her younger sister was almost inside the house. Esme was always one for dramatics, but this was against the plan. As much as this episode annoyed Tessa, it infuriated her older sister. Val marched past Tessa midway between the house and the shed. Her strides were long and angry, and the nail gun remained clutched in her hand.

Tessa quickened her pace. If Val confronted Esme without her there to buffer the exchange, things could get heated quickly.

And Val was carrying a nail gun. She wouldn't dare kill her sister with a nail to the head. Sure, they rarely agreed, but they were blood. They couldn't kill one another, could they?

Once Val's temper took hold, there was no telling what could happen.

To make matters worse, Esme's favorite hobby was pushing Val's buttons. She knew which buttons to hit, and when to hit them.

Val was the first into the house with Tessa right behind her. The inside of the farmhouse was old. The furniture was frayed around the edges. The walls needed a fresh coat of sky-blue paint. The hard wood finish peeked out from under the beige carpet in the corners where the wall met the floor.

They found Esme in the kitchen, chugging a glass of water with her bunny mask on the table.

At the first sight of her, Val tore off her mask and discarded it onto the table beside Esme's. "What the hell are you doing?"

"What am I doing? You shot a fucking nail into his hand. We don't even know if he's the right guy." Esme paced the room for added effect.

Tessa took off her mask and sucked in the old air of the kitchen. There was a hint of grease from the morning's bacon. But it was still better than what the shed offered.

Val's voice stayed surprisingly calm. "We're getting the confession out of him."

"You do realize…" Esme shifted her gaze from Tessa to Val, and back again. "Even if he's not the guy, we can't let him go? He's going to tell the cops and we'll get arrested for kidnapping and torturing him."

Val leaned against the chair at the kitchen table. "We're not letting him go. He's the guy."

Esme turned to Tessa with desperation in her eyes. "This plan is already fucked. You know that, right?"

"He's the guy." Tessa let her deciding vote hang in the air. "Esme, I get it. It's a lot. If you don't want to do it, all I ask is you dig the grave out by the trees. Val and I will handle the rest."

"We should have done what Mom instructed, and let her friends handle this." Esme grabbed her bunny mask.

"Too late." Val lowered the pig mask over her face. "No regrets."

Ever since they were children, Tessa had been assigned the role of peacemaker. Curse of the middle child. Even after the funeral, when their mother's mystery friends stayed behind to help clean the house, it was Tessa who delivered the deciding vote to hear what they had to say.

Maybe all of this *was* Tessa's fault.

Val wanted nothing to do with the two women. In her eyes it had been time for the sisters to mourn and figure out the next steps. Her voice had been adamant and simmering with a mix of exhaustion and rage. Esme welcomed the added hands to clean the house and would listen to anyone as long as they cleaned dishes and scooped casseroles into Tupperware.

Janice, the older of the two women, had pulled her auburn hair back into a ponytail and removed her jacket to reveal a leather vest, exposing her tattoo covered arms and numerous bracelets adorned with turquoise stones. As she scrubbed the hardened bits of macaroni and cheese out of a glass baking dish, she said their mother had left her and the other woman a set of instructions.

Kim, the other mystery friend, a petite Vietnamese woman in her fifties, ushered potato salad into a glass Pyrex container and said their mother wanted them to wait until she had died before arriving at the house.

Their mother had always been a straight shooter.

Janice flew in from Arizona. Kim came from Maryland. She picked up Janice from the airport. A reunion of two women who hadn't seen each other in decades.

According to Janice, when you get to be a certain age, weddings and funerals become the only times you see old friends. She fondled a towel, dried the glass dish, and casually mentioned there would have been six or seven others who would have come to pay their respects to their mother.

Kim said they didn't tell any of those people about her passing. Out of respect for the family. Besides, she said, they didn't want to make her funeral about the past.

What about her past? Tessa had asked.

Kim and Janice exchanged a look. Each woman unsure of how to proceed and hoping the other had a smooth transition. After about ten seconds of suffocating silence, Kim said the words.

Not only did the words set them on the path leading them to this night, they reshaped the sisters' perception of their mother.

Kim shifted her eyes onto the Pyrex container as she pushed the lid onto it. Without a hint of eye contact, she spoke as if delivering the secret that was eating her from the inside out.

Divinity's Reach

Five

From the way she stomped across the shed and snatched the shovel, Tessa knew her younger sister was in full pout mode. Esme's sulking was often followed by some rebellious action. As if she was ashamed she let herself act in such a childish manner, and the only way to make amends was to revolt.

Like the time she had gotten into a fight with her mother, about a month after her dad's suicide. The following Sunday, Esme descended the stairs in the navy-blue dress she reserved for weddings, and informed them she was headed to church. Her mother's disdain for organized religion was no secret among the sisters, so when she told Esme to enjoy herself, the entire kitchen fell silent. Esme, to her credit, maintained the charade for about a full month. Even went so far as to bring a Bible home. The Great Jesus Rebellion ended when her mother offered to bake her cookies so she could have a donation for the church bake sale.

Religion was much less exciting when your family supported you.

Tessa could tell Esme was seething. Esme didn't like to lose, especially when she took the moral high ground. Tessa wondered how she would rebel against this latest injustice.

Esme brushed past them and made her way out of the shed without closing the door behind her.

"I'm gonna die of tetanus," the man whimpered. But it was enough to get Tessa and Val's attention.

Tessa closed the door. "You'll be fine."

"We've got some questions for you." Val held the nail gun perpendicular to her face for added effect.

"You should know, a new guy started working at the store. Real shady guy." The man took a second to gather himself. "Works the morning and day shift. He works the weekends too."

"Let me guess," Tessa said. "Is his name John?"

The man offered no response.

"Do you really think," Val pointed the nail gun at the man, "we're stupid?"

"I'm not the guy you're looking for. I promise you."

"You know the punishment for lying." Val made her way over to the man. "I'll let you choose where this nail goes."

"You don't have to do this," he pleaded. Drool escaped his lips and found a home on his sweat stained shirt. "I'll help you find the guy you're looking for."

"Looks like it's dealer's choice," Tessa said.

Val pushed the nail gun against the man's kneecap. A familiar hiss broke the silence, quickly followed by the crack of his kneecap as the nail broke through the bone.

He screamed as the blood burst out from around the nail and peppered Val's legs. Tears streaked his face. Tessa stared at the half-exposed nail protruding from his knee. A red line appeared on his pant leg.

"Tell us about *Divinity's Reach*," Tessa said.

The man ignored her. His attention shifted from the nail in his kneecap to the one in his hand. "I need a hospital."

Tessa knew Esme had been right. They'd gone too far now. This man had to die tonight, whether he was the right guy or not. Could she live with herself if this was the wrong guy? Were they on the verge of killing some working stiff trying to make it through the day?

They needed him to confess.

"I asked you a question." Tessa made her way over to the wall and selected a ball peen hammer. "Tell us about *Divinity's Reach*."

The man spoke between sobs. "I don't know what that is."

Val exhaled as she spoke. "Yes, you do."

"No. I swear. I have no idea what you're talking about."

Tessa gave the hammer a light swing. "Tell us what you were doing in the '90s."

The man's head slumped. "I don't know what you want me to say. I was…" he stammered as he searched his memory. "I was… working construction. In New Jersey. My brother got me the job."

Val turned to face Tessa. "He's lying… again."

"I'm not lying!" he protested, his voice rising like his fear. "If I knew what you wanted to hear, I would tell you. I promise. Please. Take the nails out of me."

Val laid the nail gun on the workbench. "Tell us about Janice Bridgers. She was a runaway when you found her."

"I don't know anyone by that name."

Tessa kneeled in front of him and rested the hammer on his lap. "You know her. In the mid '90s. You met her. You recruited her. You drugged her."

"Is this some sick game? Who are you people?"

Tessa lowered her voice until it was barely more than a whisper. "Tell us about the initiation. What did you make them do before they joined your cult?"

"You think I'm a cult leader?" The man forced a chuckle. "Do I look like a cult leader to you?"

Val pulled a rusted hacksaw from the wall.

Tessa's voice was stern. "Is this funny?"

"The entire thing is absurd."

In an instant, the hammer was in Tessa's hand as she rose to her feet. Before the man could protest or turn his head, with all the force she could muster, she brought it straight into his closed mouth. His two front teeth shattered on impact and his upper lip split all the way to his nose.

He turned his head to spit out blood and his front teeth. When he turned back, Tessa could see the exposed gums where his teeth used to be. In a panic, he exhaled, and his split lip flapped outward from the rush of air. He coughed from the blood he swallowed.

Val dodged the puddle of blood on her way to the man. "Remind us of what you called the men in your cult." He remained silent. "Your disciples. Isn't that what you called them?"

Tessa studies the blood on the hammer. "Tell us how the women were expected to act."

"What did you make them do with each other?" Val paused. "And with your disciples."

"Tell us about the things they did with you," Tessa added.

The man's eyes filled with tears. The wound gave him a new lisp as he said, "This guy… not me."

Tessa's skin tingled as sweat formed. "You're not Brother John?"

A torrent of blood gushed out of the man's face as she shook his head.

"Explain why," Val paused for dramatic effect, "our mother has an entire file on you?"

The man coughed blood and let it seep out of his mouth and onto his shirt. "Maybe she's an idiot."

The two sisters turned to each other in shock before Val turned her attention back to the man. Her voice had a quality Tessa had never heard before. A disturbing mix of menace and sorrow. "Grab his fingers."

On her knees in an instant, Tessa grabbed the man's fingers on his left hand and pulled them so they were fully extended. Val brought the saw next to his index finger.

The man didn't fight.

When the teeth of the saw broke through the first layer of skin, his body tensed. With each sawing motion, blood squirted out of the cut and onto Tessa's mask. When the saw connected with bone, his body shook. The bone resisted the rusted teeth of the saw as best it could as the shed filled with the grating sound of the struggle.

Val grunted as she applied more force, determined to get the hacksaw through the bone. As the bone severed, the man emitted a pathetic scream. His flayed lips gave it an unintentional vibrato. Once through the bone, the hacksaw made quick work of the remaining skin and tissue, and soon the finger was off and in Tessa's hand for a split second before Val grabbed it from her.

The man coughed and let a line of bloodied saliva dangle from his mouth. "This night will haunt you until your last breath."

Val pointed the finger at him. "Do you remember Nadia, the Russian girl? She was only 17 when she joined *Divinity's Reach*."

"It doesn't matter how I answer." The stem of saliva broke and landed in his lap. He stared at the spot on his pants.

"You drugged her." Val jabbed the finger at him for emphasis. "And convinced her to volunteer for *The Great Vivification*. Didn't you?"

"If you say so."

Val held the finger to the light. She studied it for a moment and said, "Foxy, hold his head."

Her voice gave Tessa a reason to hesitate. Through the fox mask, she searched Val for a hint of what was to come. But Val's attention was on the finger. A theatrical display, Tessa hoped would encourage their captive to reconsider his position.

All the man did was drool blood all over himself.

Val repeated, her voice unwavering, "Hold his head."

Tessa's Air Max running shoes were heavy, as if her feet had been replaced with cinder blocks. The room spun as she made her way behind the man in the chair. A switch had flipped inside of Val. This was uncharted territory.

Was Val enjoying this?

When she arrived behind him, Tessa brought her right forearm under his chin and held his forehead in place with her other hand. The man didn't offer any resistance. Val arrived at the chair, leaned over, and said, "You lied to them about what they were eating, didn't you?"

Tessa struggled as he fought to raise his head to meet Val's eyes. He didn't speak. His desperation was replaced with the quiet calm of a man who was prepared to meet death.

Val shoved the finger into his face, centimeters from his mouth. "Since you like the taste of human flesh, open up."

He kept his mouth closed, but his flayed lips left his gums exposed.

"Open his mouth, Foxy."

Within seconds, Tessa had his mouth pried open enough for Val to shove his finger into it. He tried to spit it out, but Val covered his mouth with the palm of her hand. Blood from his split lip seeped between her fingers.

"Chew it!" Val yelled.

The man refused to chew his own finger. Tessa knew if he swallowed it, he could choke. But at least they'd be free of whatever else this night had in store for them.

End this thing before it gets worse.

"Tilt his head back, Foxy." Val's voice was sharp and commanding.

Tessa pulls back on his forehead, lifting his chin. Val punched him in the stomach. A grunt muffled against Val's palm. She punched him again, this time knocking the wind out of him. He tried to suck in air, but her palm stayed over his mouth, forcing him to breathe through his nose.

Val added more force to the hand covering his mouth. "Did he swallow it?"

His throat bulged against Tessa's wrist. "I believe so."

Val moved her hand and Tessa let go of his head. Instantly, he tried to cough and dislodge the finger in his throat. Specks of blood flew out of his mouth. He tried clearing his throat, but the air wheezed out of him.

His face turned purple. "Water. Water."

Neither of the sisters moved. His eyes were wide with panic. He cleared his throat in an act of desperation. The cough vibrated against the finger blocking his airways. His body rocked back and forth as he tried to clear the obstruction.

Another cough. This one was abrupt, but it freed enough room in his throat for more air to break through. Realizing the tables could be turning, he cleared his throat again. This time with all the force he could muster. The finger ejected out of his mouth, bounced off Val's leg, and landed on the floor by her feet, covered in mucus and blood. The man sucked in as much air as his lungs could handle.

Val marched to the nail gun on the workbench. "Take off his pants."

"You can't be serious." Tessa straightened her back to face her sister.

Val grabbed the nail gun. "Take them off." Her tone was controlled but packed enough aggression that Tessa moved to the front of the man and kneeled.

Warm feces and hot urine assaulted Tessa's nostrils. "He pissed *and* shit himself."

Val arrived by her sister. "Pants and underwear."

The man's body quivered as Tessa grasped the waistline of his pants. She undid the button and lowered the zipper. The fetid contents of the underwear slapped her nostrils. Tessa turned her head, hoping for a brief whiff of fresh air.

But none came.

Her fingers slipped between the underwear and his skin. As she prepared to yank his pants and underwear down, her fingers slid into something moist and creamy. Her body convulsed. It could only be one thing and it triggered her gag reflex. The softness enveloped her fingers with the warmth of pureed baby food. Vomit rose in her throat, but she choked it back.

Tessa held her breath and yanked the man's pants past his butt as quickly as possible. She didn't stop until they were around his ankles. Her fingers came free of the waste, but they remained covered in a brownish green paste. While rising to her feet, she caught a glimpse of the mess he had been sitting in for hours. Long enough for the edges to dry and form a crust.

"Did you ever go by the name of Brother John?" Val checked to make sure the nail gun had ammunition.

"I already answered you."

Tessa stared at the nastiness covering her fingers. This is not how their night was supposed to go. Val had taken things to an extreme level. Who had she become?

Val kneeled by the man, unaffected by the odor intensifying since its release into the open air. She took a moment to ogle the feces smeared all over his penis and scrotum. "He still won't confess to his sins."

The muscles in Tessa's body twitched. There was a gleam in Val's eye. Almost an excitement for whatever she was about to do. A realization poured over Tessa like a bucket of cold water.

Her sister *was* enjoying this.

Tessa tried to speak, but her voice caught in her throat.

With a complete disregard for the feces coating the man's privates, Val grabbed his scrotum and pinned it against this right thigh.

The man yelled. "No!"

Val held the nail gun flush against the man's sack. The whistle from the gun was quick and stealthy.

He emitted a primal scream, shuddering the walls of the shed. Seconds later, he passed out. Either from shock, exhaustion, or loss of blood. For all Tessa knew, it could have been all three.

Val admired her handy work as she rose to her feet, her hand covered in the same filth as Tessa's. What she left behind was the man's scrotum pinned to the side of his thigh with a bloody nail.

Tessa's throat was so dry it cracked as she spoke. "Outside. Now."

Once outside, Tessa headed straight for the faucet connected to the side of the shed. She used her foot to turn it on and let the water run over her hands. Tessa could hear Val's footsteps, heavy and plodding behind her. "When we go back in there, we're killing him. No more torture." The footsteps stopped. Tessa turned to see Val staring off into the distance. "Do you hear me? It's gone too far, Val. We're done."

Val raised a lone, poo covered finger, and pointed at the opposite side of the yard, by the edge of the tree line. "Where is she?"

Tessa's knees went weak. Across the yard was a barely dug grave. Beside it, stuck in the ground, sat the shovel.

Esme was nowhere to be found.

Six

Val was already headed towards the surrounding woods when she said, "You search the house, I'll take the woods."

Two steps into the house and Tessa froze, listening. There was nothing but still air in the musty old farmhouse their mother had died in. Tessa ventured deeper into the house, arriving in the kitchen. In the middle sat the kitchen table, the one her dad had built when the family expanded to five people. Now the fifth member of the family was missing.

The house was cold and empty. Devoid of love and laughter. Memories flooded Tessa's brain. There was the side of the cabinet where Val fell and cracked her head open. To this day, her scar remained hidden under her hair.

The stove top where Mother would use the hot comb to straighten their hair on Sunday mornings. As children, they always wondered why their family never attended church on Sundays. After meeting Janice and Kim, they knew the answer

Tessa stood and stared at the second floor. How many times had she travelled these stairs? Racing out the door to catch her big sister. Each step had its own quirk. She knew which stairs had been replaced by her father, which stairs weren't the right size, which ones creaked if you put too much weight on the left side, which would give a little when you pressed on it.

Once upstairs, she called out, "Esme!" When there was no answer, she pushed open the first door on the right and stepped into Val's room.

Empty.

Tessa clenched her jaw. They had been so careful. There was no way they could have been followed. And if they had, why would the person let them commit all those horrible acts before kidnapping one of them? A coincidence seemed too far-fetched. Who would kidnap her?

Tessa was grinding her teeth, the way she always did when things were spinning out of control. In the 800, when the lead runners pulled away, she would grind her teeth and dig in. Lactic acid would pulse through her legs, but she always fought through it.

She left Val's room and stared at the door across the hall. If Esme was in the bathroom, they'd spend the rest of their lives laughing about it. But Tessa knew she wasn't in there. As her hand moved to the doorknob, Esme's scream reverberated off the walls. It came from outside, and was still loud enough to send Tessa's heart into overdrive.

Tessa descended the stairs two at a time and nearly tumbled. She braced herself against the wall and went straight for the kitchen.

Another scream.

Spurred on by adrenaline and fear, Tessa grabbed the butcher knife out of the block. The desperation of the screams meant her sister was in trouble. She bounded across the living room in four steps and was out the door in seconds.

Another scream. This one was cut short as Tessa stepped out of the farmhouse.

The man, bloodied and naked below the waist, with his torn ball sack open, was right behind Esme as they both limped out of the shed and towards the house. The outside of her left leg was covered in blood.

The ball peen hammer swung wildly in his hand.

Tessa was halfway across the front porch when he tackled Esme. His blood, feces, and saliva covered her as he climbed on top of her. Her hands met his face, covering her fingers with blood from his split lip. His eyes were wild as the moon glistened against the aged chrome of the raised hammer.

Halfway across the yard, Tessa's heart sank.

Esme tried to scream again, but the man stifled it with his other palm.

In an instant, he brought the hammer onto her head. The crack of her skull was so loud it reverberated off the siding of the farmhouse.

Her body went limp.

The man brought the hammer onto her skull again with another sickening crunch.

Val, in a full sprint, appeared out of nowhere and tackled him with enough force to launch them both three feet away from Esme.

Tessa checked her pulse. Time slowed to a standstill as she moved her finger under Esme's nose to confirm what her heart already knew to be true. Her final act of rebellion against her sisters had been to free their captive.

Val was the first on her feet. In one step she was beside the man, who was on his hands and knees. She kicked him across the face and his body flipped over so he landed on his back.

Tessa blinked and a tear escaped from the corner of her eye. She clutched the butcher knife and turned to join her sister.

Val raised her boot over the man's face to crush his skull with her heel. Before she could cave in his head, he slammed the hammer into her other knee with all the force he could muster. Val doubled over, and the man bludgeoned her across the nose with the hammer. Her entire body soared backwards. Blood exploded out of her twisted nose.

Before he could get to his feet, Tessa jammed the knife into his rib cage and twisted the blade. Their bodies close enough for her to lean into his ear and whisper, "Die asshole, die."

Tessa took pleasure in watching as blood oozed out from between the man's teeth, until the cold of the hammer barreled into the side of her skull, knocking her to the ground in a haze of unconsciousness.

Blood warmed the side of Tessa's face. When her vision returned, the man was on top of Val, using the knife to cut her stomach open. Tessa tried to rise, but again, she succumbed to the darkness.

The man yelled, "Look what you're making me do. Look what you turned me into." Tessa pried her eyes open enough to see him pulling Val's intestines out of her stomach.

The hammer remained on the ground, right where he left it.

He didn't notice Tessa as she crawled towards the hammer, too busy cramming Val's intestines into her mouth.

"Eat, bitch. Eat!" The man's wails were desperate and unhinged.

He was right. They changed him. Whether or not he was Brother John didn't matter. He was rabid. An unhinged beast wanting more than to kill them. He wanted to torture and defile them.

Same as they had done to him.

Determination beat back the impending darkness and Tessa grabbed the hammer. Her legs wobbled as she rose to her feet and stumbled towards the man straddling her sister. As she got a closer view, the scene churned her stomach. He laughed and cackled as he pulled another handful out of Val's exposed stomach, shoving it into her mouth.

Clarity rushed back as Tessa arrived behind him. "Hey." He turned to face her. Weary from a night of torture and blood loss, he only smiled as Tessa broke his skull open with the hammer. His body flopped to the ground next to Val's.

He was still, but Tessa wasn't taking any chances. She took aim and slammed the hammer into his forehead with enough force it remained lodged in the hole she created. After some twisting and jiggling, Tessa pulled the hammer out and took aim once again. This time, she used the hammer to cave in his face, right under his left eye.

Before she knew it, Tessa was hammering the man's head and face, the ball peen peppering him with holes and indents. When the skull shattered and broke away to expose his brain, she decided it was time to stop. The hammer fell from her hand, and she went to see about Val.

There was no need to check her pulse, or to slide a finger under her nose. "What did we do, Val?" Tessa used the back of her hand to wipe away a tear. "What did we do?"

SEVEN

Lactic acid sets in when muscles try to break down carbohydrates without enough oxygen to help in the process. As a result, Tessa's muscles were heavy and lethargic. Her hands were raw and callused. The first hole, the one for Brother John, was half completed by her sister. It was tiring work, but her body was used to physical exertion.

The second grave told Tessa how much she had let herself go. She had stopped running when she got the news about her mother. Her last six-mile jaunt had done nothing more than stress her out as funeral arrangements hung over her head, and the constant fighting between Val and Esme had become unbearable. Even music had done nothing to supplant the misery of those last few jogs.

It had been months since she had a good run. And now here she was, huffing and puffing after digging two graves—one for Brother John, and another, bigger grave for both of her sisters. It was crude, and her sisters deserved better than a shared grave, but the sun would be out soon, and time was of the essence. She had to get these bodies in the ground and hit the road.

She took a moment to lean on the handle of the shovel and suck in the cold air. Her shirt was drenched with blood and sweat. The family plot of land was littered with dead bodies and empty graves.   This hole was deep enough for her sisters. Besides, morning would be here in an hour or so. She left the shovel in place, looped her arms under the man's shoulders, and dragged him to his grave. He was heavy and left a trail of blood. The digging had worn her out, but dragging this two-hundred-pound man to the hole was nothing short of torture. Her legs ached and her head throbbed. No matter how much air she sucked in, it wasn't enough for her lungs. At the grave, she dropped him on the edge, took a seat on the ground next to his body, and used her feet to coerce him into his final resting place. He landed in the hole face first.

Tessa laid in the grass and stared into the clear night sky. Her chest heaved as she sucked in all the wind she could get. The blood on her face had dried to the point of cracking when she moved her eyes or jaw. She attempted to identify the constellations, but quit after a few minutes. Esme could pick out the little dipper, the belt, and all the other ones Tessa failed to identify. As little girls, they would sit out under the stars and fantasize about going to other countries and having adventures. Esme was fascinated by Egypt with its Pyramids and hieroglyphs. She would talk her favourite sister's ears off for hours under the stars, with facts both interesting and mundane.

Under these same stars, they had both made plans to escape this life and get as far away from this farmhouse as possible. Escape their mother and their older sister. Tessa had made it as far as Temple University, some six hours away. And when she graduated, she moved to the city.

Esme never made it out. She had struggled in school, and didn't excel at any skills to help her get out. Instead, she stayed in the house and seethed as Tessa moved on.

But in death, their mother had not only managed to reunite the sisters, but forced her middle child back into the vortex.

In the end, their mother always seemed to get her way.

Rest time was over. Tessa needed to get these bodies in the ground and covered with dirt. How long had she been lying here?

Val would be first. She was the heavier of the two, best to drag her into the hole while she had a bit more energy. As Tessa dragged Val towards the hole, she couldn't help but smile. What would their mother say if she was watching Tessa right now? Her least favorite daughter dragging her favorite into a crudely dug hole where they'd have to rest until some dog or coyote came around and started investigating. Their mother was a woman of action, so she'd be proud of the way they marched into Allentown and kidnapped Brother John. She'd be proud of the retribution they exacted on the man who did such vile things to her.

But she would not be happy about how sloppy they were. She'd suck her teeth, the way she did when she was disappointed, watching them bicker amongst themselves when there was a job to do. And worst of all, her favorite two daughters were dead because of their lack of focus.

She would be none too pleased with the culmination of events.

Val's intestines hung out her open stomach and dragged along the ground between her legs as Tessa dragged the body to the edge of the shallow grave and pushed her in. She landed on her back, with a clear view of the night sky. Ironic, considering Val never showed any interest in nature, or the heavens above. No matter. She was about to have her view obstructed by dirt and rocks.

Val and Mother butted heads almost daily. They were the most alike, so they were destined to lock horns. Val inherited her short fuse from Mother along with her take charge demeanor. The stubbornness was all Mother as well. It's why they fought the way they did, but it's also why they were the closest. There's a bond between mother and first born. And the more children there are, the stronger the bond.

Tessa grabbed Esme by the legs and drug her body towards the grave. Val may have acted like their mother, but it was Esme who looked the most like her. The skin tone and those elevated, sharp cheekbones. Those dark, foreboding eyes. When Esme was still an infant, Val and Tessa would sit and watch as their mother doted over the new arrival. The two older sisters knew this baby was going to be their mother's favorite.

The truth of the matter never bothered Tessa. In her eyes, there was no difference between being the second of two children, or the third of three children. Either way, she was still last.

Val, on the other hand, didn't take kindly to the new threat. She was not happy about having some of her standing being usurped by this little girl who was hoarding all of Mother's attention.

And now, the rivals can lay together in this hole under the stars on the family's plot of land. Val's plan brought them here. And, of course, Esme's rebellion monkey-wrenched the entire situation. This was the last time the youngest and oldest would do battle.

Staying true to form, it was the middle sister who cleaned the mess.

When the first load of dirt hit Brother John, Tessa paused. Not only should she be burying the three dead bodies, but she should also be burying as much of the evidence as possible. The hammer. The saw. The knife.

And where was Brother John's finger? It must still be in the shed where he spit it out.

His pants must be in there also.

Tessa gathered the hammer and the knife and tossed them into the hole on top of Brother John.

Inside the shed, there was still a hint of feces and urine, but it was mixed with a dampness she hadn't detected before. Perhaps it had always been in the air, masked by Brother John's soiled pants.

On the floor by the overturned chair was the finger, sitting in filth, blood, and who knows what else. Tessa plucked it off the ground using her thumb and index finger. The hacksaw was only a few feet away. She grabbed it as well.

The man's pants laid in a crumbled heap on the floor by the chair. Tessa grabbed them, and avoiding all the brown smears, she pulled out a wallet. Inside were eleven dollars in cash, prepaid gas cards, and a driver's license. She studied the Pennsylvania license and a plan materialized. Her hands went back into his other pockets, careful to evade the brown cream crusted in various sections. When she flipped the pants over, she heard an unmistakable sound.

Keys.

In an instant, she had the keys in her hand. Keys and a driver's license changed things. She would still leave, but now she had a new destination.

Tessa marched out of the shed and across the yard. The hacksaw and finger were bundled in the pants cradled in her arms. She tossed them into the hole with Brother John, and set about filling the hole with dirt. She worked at a feverish pace. Sweat covered her forehead and made its way into her eyes. Her discoveries fueled her with a new sense of purpose.

After these holes were filled, she was going to shower, hop in the van, and drive to Allentown. She was going to the man's house to find proof he was the cult leader who brainwashed and abused her mother.

Eight

Raised on collard greens and ham hocks, outcast to her mother, specimen in need of molding to her father, Tessa was the last one standing. The irony wasn't lost on her.

Brother John ruined her mother before any of the girls were even born. Took whatever she had been and made her vengeful and paranoid. And this new incarnation met and married a man, settled on the family plot, and had three girls.

Tessa gripped the steering wheel of the rental van as the morning sun presented itself, like the jaundiced eye of an exhausted demon. Traffic slowed her pace, but Tessa wasn't in a rush. Brother John's place wasn't going anywhere.

Forty miles to Allentown.

Did her mother's secret worm its way into her dad's ear? Secrets are hard to keep. Especially when they define who you are as a person. Was her dad's suicide because of Brother John? Sure, it would be indirect, but still?

Her mother's body gave out on her. Her dad ate a shotgun shell in the same bathtub her mother had bathed her daughters in. And now her sisters were gone. Like an avatar with a grudge against her family, Brother John finished the job he started when he coerced their mother from her job at the diner all those years ago. The decimation of her family was his magnum opus.

Why was she suppressing a smile?

How long had she been calling him Brother John? She hadn't seen any evidence he was the cult leader. He hadn't admitted to it. In the pit of her stomach, Tessa knew the answer. She didn't want to admit it, but the answer lurked. The pain had been in the back of her throat since her sister used the nail gun on his sack.

Knowing their victim was Brother John would bridge the gap between who she thought she was, and who she truly was. The things they did to the man were ungodly. But if Janice and Kim's stories were true, he deserved what he got.

If the stories were true.

Of course the stories were true. The details were so vivid, there was no way they could have been lies. Janice told them of how Mother had found her and took her to the diner for scrambled eggs, bacon, and a short stack of pancakes. Mother asked her where she was headed, and when Janice didn't have an answer, she invited her to come to the commune.

Twenty miles to Allentown, Tessa could hear the empty Red Bull cans rolling into each other as she braked for the morning gridlock.

Kim was only fifteen when Brother John found her working the parking lot of a truck stop. Desperate to escape her pimp and a life of beatings, she hopped in his car, and an hour later, she was introduced to her mother. For three years, her mother kept Brother John and the other men of *Divinity's Reach* away from her. But at eighteen, she had her Blossoming.

Over tea and pound cake, the two women recounted how her mother, after finding out what they had eaten at the Vivification, instructed Janice and Kim to find all the women they trusted. Between sips of chamomile, they told the story of how her mother stole money for the bus fair while Janice and Kim stole food and water for the journey.

In the middle of the night, the eight women fled. Racing through the woods, some of them barefoot, the women didn't stop until they were at a bus stop. Her mother gave each of the women enough money for a one-way ticket to anywhere they wanted to go. It was the last time they saw her alive.

Janice had choked back tears as she told the sisters about the women they didn't trust.

The women they left behind.

A decade or so later, the women of *Divinity's Reach* began getting in touch with each other. Sharing updates. Having some tough conversations about why some were chosen to escape and others weren't. Stories came out about the last weeks of *Divinity's Reach*. Brother John's paranoia grew. His disciples bickered amongst each other about how to handle the situation. Women were raped. Beaten. Tortured. And one day, Brother John and his disciples were gone. Once again, those women had been left behind.

Janice, Kim, and a few of the other women had found information on her mother and got in touch. But she never answered the calls. Never replied to the emails.

Until she received her diagnoses and decided it was time to tell them her plan.

Ten miles to Allentown.

By chance, a liquor store in Allentown had been robbed. And when the news footage circulated through news outlets and social media, Mother knew the face of the cashier. It was the man who made her do vile, sordid acts in the name of community and love. The man who made her do things she never knew she was capable of doing.

Janice and Kim had told the sisters their mother had stashed the address and the picture in her bedroom. The sisters were to find them, deliver the information to Janice and Kim, who would tell the other women. Mother's plan had been for all the women, together, to kidnap their abuser and make him suffer.

It was Val who said the sisters should do this. After all, it was their mother who devised the plan.

According to Val, their mother didn't trust some of these women when it was time to escape, so why should they trust them now? What if one of them went to the police? Val didn't have much faith in the justice system. Especially when it came to women accusing a white man of crimes from thirty years ago.

The GPS said Tessa was only five minutes away.

Tessa had her reservations, but it was Esme who protested the loudest. The women should do it, she proclaimed. They were the ones who suffered.

But Val was right. It had been their mother who found him. Tessa sided with Val, and two hours later they had a fully formed plan.

Now Esme and Val were dead, and Tessa was sitting in a rented van across from an apartment complex, hoping to find proof the guy she and her sisters murdered was the former cult leader.

The justification for this enterprise was a little half baked. Her sick mother saw a guy on TV and now her sisters are dead and she can never go home again.

She should save the trouble and turn herself in to the police.

The morning sun forced Tessa to squint as she arrived at the front of the brick complex with the white shudders. She tapped the fob against the lock box and the front door hummed and buzzed as it opened.

Apartment 209 had to be on the second floor, so Tessa marched through the hall until she found the stairwell. With her heart ready to explode out of her chest, she took the stairs two at a time. Her hamstrings screamed from the soreness of a night of fighting and grave digging. The entire building smelled of abandoned plumbing projects.

The apartment revealed itself in the middle of the hallway, two doors from the smashed cockroach in the middle of the hall. Brother John's keys were heavy and loud, but after trying four of the keys, she found the correct one and unlocked the door. She entered the apartment and her stomach sank. The place was nothing like she imagined it would be.

It was cheap and tidy.

Nothing in this place could have cost more than two hundred dollars.

There wasn't much in the way of a design aesthetic. White walls gave way to hardwood floors. All the furniture was black.

And it was all pristine.

This couldn't be the lair of a sexual predator who prayed on women. The den of a man who worked the night shift at a liquor store.

What did she expect? Body parts dangling from the ceiling? She opened the refrigerator. There was a gallon of milk, a few containers of Chinese take-out, and more condiments than any one person could possibly need.

Who needs three different kinds of hoisin sauce?

A lump was forming in her throat. Beads of sweat formed at the top of her forehead. They had the wrong guy. She made the decision. If she couldn't find proof, she would leave here and turn herself in to the police. Tessa knew she could go on the run and evade the cops for some time, but eventually they would catch her.

After what they did to that man, they deserved what they got. Tessa deserved to spend the rest of her life being treated like the animal she didn't realize she was.

How could they have done this?

Tessa figured she might as well search the place. Otherwise, what was the point of the four-hour drive?

If nothing else, she could see if the man had a family. So, when her trial came around, she would have some idea of what she was in for.

The tears.

The emotional pleas.

The shouts of murderer.

Tessa's throat was dry. Gasping for air, she ripped open cabinet after cabinet until she found the one with drinking glasses. She selected the one with the least soap scum, ran it under the tap, and gulped it so fast it hurt her throat. Doubled over, Tessa stared into the empty sink as she caught her breath. Summoning whatever resolve she could muster, she trudged towards the only bedroom in the apartment.

Senior year at Temple, Tessa's longest relationship was with a software engineer who was obsessed with first person shooters. He had a top-of-the-line computer with dual monitors. In the midst of a heated game session, she overheard him bragging about his five-thousand dollar-graphics card. The CPU he had was the biggest she'd ever seen. His keyboard looked like a relic from the future. One evening, he told her she could use his computer to send an email to her professor. Tessa was too intimidated to touch any part of his futuristic supercomputer. In the end, she dictated the email to her boyfriend.

An equally impressive workstation occupied half of the bedroom.

Tessa dropped to her knees and bent over to have a look under the bed. To her disappointment, there wasn't a single thing under there. Not a shoe box or condom wrapper.

Who was this guy?

More and more, Tessa felt like she knew who he wasn't.

Her desperation grew by the second. She stomped across the room and flung open the closet door. On the right side of the closet were the shirts. Arranged by color. On the left side were the pants, also arranged by color.

This man didn't own any suits. Or ties.

Tessa pushed aside the shirts, hunting for evidence to ease the surge of guilt coursing through her body. One of the shirts grabbed her attention. Her knees became weak as she read the words plastered across the chest.

Allentown Ecumenical Food Bank.

He volunteered at a food bank?

Tessa retched. Her hands covered her mouth as she sprinted across the hall and into the bathroom. What exploded out of her and into the toilet was pure liquid. It was warm enough to burn her throat as it evacuated her body. When the torrent of stomach acid and Red Bull was over, she sat back on the cold linoleum. She needed to rest for a few minutes before driving to the Allentown police station and turning herself in.

Her sisters had died for nothing.

And now she was going to spend the rest of her days in a cell.

Tessa dragged herself out of the bathroom and back into the main section of the apartment. When was the last time she ate? What was the last thing she ate? When she stopped to get the Red Bulls, she didn't buy any food. She was too worried about falling asleep at the wheel. She'd been running on adrenaline for, what, twelve hours?

She plopped onto the couch, and the moment her butt hit the cushion, exhaustion covered her like a warm blanket. Maybe she could take a quick nap, a quick refresh for when she turned herself in. There would be hundreds of questions. She needed to be ready.

It's not like the man was coming home, and there were no signs of anyone else living here. She took her shoes off and laid on the couch. She could smell her feet. They were sweaty from all the activity of the previous night. But they weren't the only things she smelled.

She was in desperate need of soap and water.

But for now, she needed rest. When she awoke, she could take a shower. Make herself presentable for her mugshot.

As sleep took hold, her eyes focused on the middle section of the TV stand beside the DVD player. It was one of those flip book style cases made for holding CDs and DVDs.

Who still owned CDs?

Tessa was so tired she didn't even stand. She half-rolled, half-scooted across the hardwood floor until her body arrived close enough for her to pull out the case.

This man loved mobster movies. All the classics were there. Page after page of mobster movies.

Donnie Brasco.

Goodfellas.

Casino.

Once Upon a Time in America.

There were three pages of mob movies. But on the fourth page, she found burned DVDs.

All of them were labeled with a black sharpie. Each of the labels was a name. She didn't recognize any of the names on the page, but this discovery was enough to make her hands shake.

She selected the first one. The name scrawled across it read *Clara.* She turned on the DVD player and it inhaled the first disc. Tessa found the remote by the TV. She turned it on, and after cycling through the various

HDMI outputs, she found the correct one for the DVD player.

What appeared on screen was a scene from the late nineties. A woman in her early twenties, staring straight into the camera. Her pale skin was healthy and vibrant. Her big brown eyes were a mix of madness and joy. "We're all so excited, we don't know what to do. I know, for me, this is my home now, and I can't wait to experience my new family members. There's something about what we have here. It's so…" She looks away and brushes away a tear. "I want to give myself to *Divinity's Reach*. I'm ready."

Tessa's jaw fell open. Her posture straightened and the tears flowed. Her finger ejected the disc from the DVD player. Excitement swelled inside her as she flipped to the next page. One disc in particular caught her eye. The label read, *Kim*'s *Blossoming*. She pulled it out of the sleeve and crammed it into the DVD player.

When the image came on screen, it almost gave Tessa motion sickness. It was a jittery handheld shot. Walls. Floor. Ceiling. Each shot lasted one or two seconds. The framing spun like the inside of a plane barreling towards the earth.

But the audio was what stiffened her back.

Men groaned and women moaned. There was the sound of sweaty flesh slapping together.

Tessa recognized the sound.

It was the sound of bodies colliding.

Sweaty bodies doing whatever was necessary to pleasure other bodies.

When the camera got oriented, the screen filled with a mass of bodies. There must have been fifteen to twenty men and women. All naked and sweaty. Every orifice was filled with a tongue, or a cock, or fingers. Lips moved from one person's body part to another person's mouth. It didn't matter who was inside of who. They moved freely from person to person. Their bodies glistened and their eyes glassed over.

Amongst the bodies were two black women. One of them had to be Tessa's mother, but both women's faces were obscured by the rhythmic thrusts of two different men's hips.

Tessa ejected the disc and flipped through the case until she found a disc titled *Vivification*. She stared at it for a moment, unsure if she could stomach the contents. She made her decision. The disc found its way into the player and the screen filled with the image of about twenty people enjoying a meal at picnic tables. The table was full of salads, bread, pitchers with a red drink, and grilled meat.

Meat.

Tessa gagged. She knew what they were eating.

At the head of the table, a man stood and tapped the side of his glass with his fork. This was the same man in the faded picture Tessa had carried for them to use as a reference.

Brother John.

Tessa's face was covered with tears. Her sisters hadn't died in vain. For once, her mother would be proud of her. Not only did they get the guy and kill him, but Tessa confirmed he was the right guy.

Brother John smiled at his congregation and said, "This is more than a meal. This communion is a reminder of the sacrifices we are willing to make for each other. The sacrifices we are willing to make for the common good."

Tessa ejected the disc. Her eyes filled. They got the right guy. There's no need to turn herself in.

Instead, she was going to run.

She'd need a new identity. She'd need to dye her hair. Maybe she could get a passport under a fake name and leave the country. She snatched the remote to turn off the TV.

Her fingerprints were all over the place.

Okay. New plan. First, a nap. She'd need to retrace her steps and wipe this place clean. She'd take a shower, freshen up, and hit the road.

She could worry about ditching the rental van later. It wasn't due back until tomorrow anyway.

The important thing was, she found the evidence she needed to live guilt free.

So why was she staring at this case of DVDs? Curiosity forced her to turn the page. She scanned the discs inside. She turned the page again and froze.

The disc in the bottom corner read, *Rhonda's Ascension.*

Her brain implored her to close the case and keep going. She didn't need to know what her mother's ascension was.

But she needed to know as much of this story as possible. Her sisters died for this.

They also killed for this.

This was a terrible idea. She knew it. But still. Eventually, she would watch all of these. There was no way she was leaving this case here. And if the case was with her as she lived off grid, or hid out, or did whatever the future held, she would have to watch all these discs.

Tessa wiped the tears from her cheeks. On the screen, a naked woman lay passed out on a bed in a nondescript room. Her pale skin was bruised, and her long black hair covered her face.

Into the frame stepped Tessa's mother. But this wasn't the version of her she remembered. This version was young and beautiful, with a wild look in her eyes. She was dressed in a robe as she got into the bed above the unconscious woman's head.

A naked man strutted into frame. His build was average at best. A little extra weight, but at one time he had a gym routine.

It was Brother John.

He stared at the passed-out woman as he worked up an erection. When he took a step towards the woman, Rhonda leaned over and spread the woman's legs apart and guided him into her.

The woman moaned as the man slowly thrust himself in and out of her.

Mother pinned the woman's shoulders and said, "It'll be over soon, honey."

The woman came to and shrieked. She tried to fight Brother John off, but Tessa's mother kept her pinned to the bed.

Brother John continued to thrust in and out as the woman screamed.

Tessa yanked the disc out of the player and let it drop to the hardwood floor with a clang echoing in her ears. She fell onto the floor and stared at the ceiling. One question remained.

Did she still need to wipe her fingerprints from the apartment?

Fingerprints wouldn't matter if she turned herself in.

Laying on the floor of Brother John's apartment, Tessa laughed until her face hurt.

Then she cried until she passed out.

THE END

SIGN UP FOR MY AUTHOR NEWSLETTER

Be the first to learn about Eric Williford's new releases and receive exclusive content!

https://thedefpix.com/pages/connect

www.ingramcontent.com/pod-product-compliance
Lightning Source LLC
Chambersburg PA
CBHW062145150726
47991CB00006B/2183